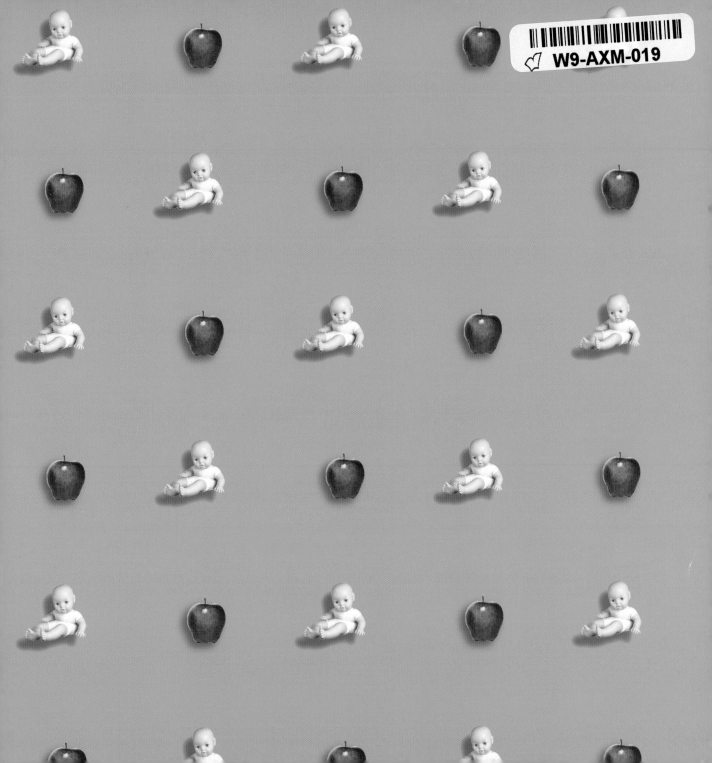

Look What I See!
Where Can I Be?
At Home

by Dia L. Michels

Photographs by
Michael J.N. Bowles

Platypus Media, LLC
Washington, DC
2002

For Tony,
who makes our house
a home

Enjoy these other *Look What I See!* books by Dia L. Michels

In the Neighborhood
With My Animal Friends
In China
At the Synagogue

Activity Guide available at PlatypusMedia.com

Library of Congress Cataloging-in-Publication Data

Michels, Dia L.
   At home / by Dia L. Michels.
       p. cm. — (Look what I see! where can I be? ; 2)
   Summary: By viewing a detail from a photograph that is revealed on the following
page, the reader is invited to guess in which part of her home Baby has awakened.
       ISBN 1-930775-06-7 (alk. paper)
       [1. Home—Fiction. 2. Babies—Fiction. 3. Family life—Fiction.] I. Title.
PZ7.M58l7 At 2002
[E]—dc21   2002016981

Platypus Media, LLC
627 A Street, NE
Washington, DC 20002
PlatypusMedia.com

1 2 3 4 5 6 7 8 9

Platypus Media is committed to the promotion and protection of breastfeeding.
We donate six percent of our profits to breastfeeding organizations.

Series editor: Ellen E.M. Roberts, Where Books Begin, New York, NY
Project management: Maureen Graney, Blackberry Press, Washington, DC
Book design: Douglas Wink, Inkway Graphics, Santa Fe, NM
Production consultant: Kathy Rosenbloom, New York, NY
Additional photography: Stuart Hovell, Motophoto Capitol Hill, Washington, DC,
and Peter Wang, Redstone, Inc., New York, NY

Acknowledgments
The author would like to thank the Miller Vizas family, the Deutsch family,
and the Kennon family, all of Washington, DC, and the Strong family of Upper
Marlboro, MD, for so generously sharing their homes. She would also like to
thank Dr. John C. Meyer, Marymont Animal Hospital, Silver Spring, MD, for his
sweet kittens.

Manufactured in the United States of America.

There is so much to see
at home with my family.

On Monday,
I fell asleep in my swing.

When I woke up,
I saw a bright tower.

Where was I?

In the
playroom.

On Tuesday,
I fell asleep
in my bouncy seat.

When I woke up,
I saw an apple flower.

Where was I?

In the kitchen.

On Wednesday,
I fell asleep
in my baby bundler.

When I woke up,
I saw a steam engine.

Where was I?

In the backyard.

I never know what I will see
at home with my family.

On Thursday,
I fell asleep
in my baby seat.

When I woke up,
I saw a rubber duckie.

Where was I?

In the
bathroom.

On Friday,
I fell asleep in my basket.

When I woke up,
I saw gray whiskers.

Where was I?

In the living room.

On Saturday,
I fell asleep on
a pillow.

When I woke up,
I saw a thumb.

Where was I?

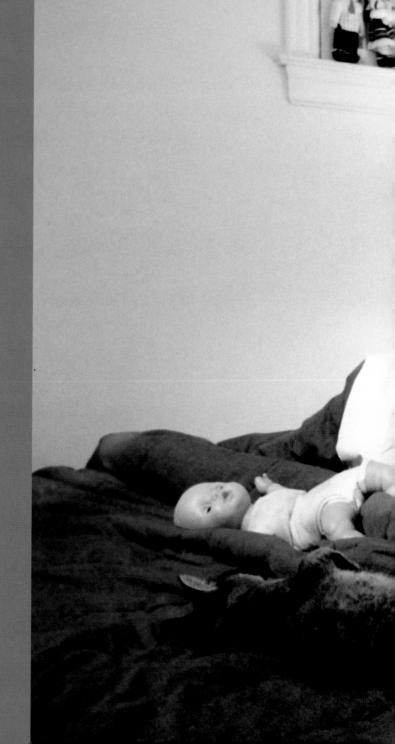

In the bedroom.

On Sunday,
I fell asleep
in my brother's lap.

When I woke up,
I saw a mommy platypus
cuddling her baby.

Where was I?

Safe and warm
by my brother's
side.

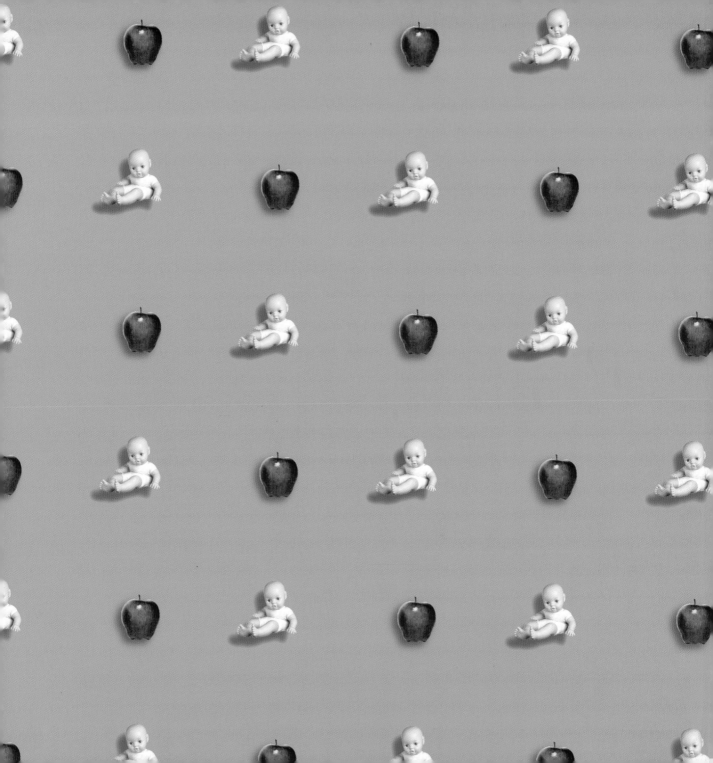